Usborne
Children's
Chocolate
Cookbook

Fiona Patchett

Designed by Nancy Leschnikoff,
Louise Flutter & Helen Edmonds

Illustrated by Jessie Eckel
Edited by Abigail Wheatley
Photography by Howard Allman
Recipe consultant: Catherine Atkinson

Contents

You'll find the recipe for these chocolate orange cookies on pages 10-11.

Find out how to make chocolate curls on page 33.

The recipe for this hot chocolate is on pages 40-41.

Getting started

The tips on this page will help you to get to grips with some chocolate cooking basics. Once you've read through them, you can start cooking.

Before you start

Before you start cooking, read the recipe carefully and check you've got all the ingredients and equipment. Always remember to wash your hands before you start.

Types of chocolate

All the recipes in this book are made with plain, milk or white chocolate, or with cocoa powder. Pages 56-57 explain about different types of chocolate, to help you to decide which one to use. On pages 58-61, you can find out about the history of chocolate and how it is made.

Food allergies

If have a food allergy or intolerance, or are cooking for someone who has, you'll find information in this book to help you. Recipes that contain nuts are clearly marked. Ingredients lists show which ingredients can be swapped for allergy-free alternatives. And on page 64 you can find out which recipes are suitable for allergy sufferers.

Weighing and measuring

Always measure ingredients accurately and use the size and shape of cake tin the recipe says.

The recipes in this book show two different types of weights. Use either, but don't swap between them. Measure small amounts with spoons, or measuring spoons if you have them. The ingredients should lie level with the top of the spoon.

For very small amounts of dry ingredients such as salt or spices, you only need a pinch. A pinch is the amount you can pick up between your thumb and first finger.

You'll find a recipe for chocolate cupcakes on pages 12-13.

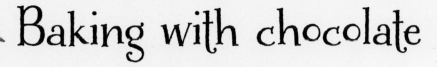

Baking with chocolate

Tips for baking with chocolate

The secret of baking is to measure everything very accurately and do exactly what the recipe says – otherwise your cakes or cookies might not turn out quite right.

Lining a tray or tin

1 Put the tin or tray on some baking parchment. Draw around it. Cut out the shape, cutting just inside the line.

2 Grease the tin or tray (see right). Put the parchment shape in the bottom of the tin or tray.

Greasing a tray or tin

1 Use a paper towel to scoop up a little softened butter or cooking oil.

2 Wipe the paper towel over the tin or tray, so it's thinly covered with butter or oil.

Your oven

All ovens are different – yours may cook things more quickly or slowly than the recipe says. If you're using a fan oven, shorten the cooking time or lower the temperature – the oven manual will help you with this.

Bake things in the middle of the oven. Arrange the oven shelves before you turn on the oven. Only open the oven door when the cooking time is up, or if you think something might be burning.

Sifting

1 Put the ingredients you need to sift in a sieve. Hold the sieve over a bowl. Tap the sieve, so the ingredients fall through.

2 If there are lumps left in the sieve (of cocoa or icing sugar, for example), squash them through with the back of a spoon.

Butter, margarine & spread

When a recipe says to use softened butter, leave it at room temperature for an hour before you start cooking. Only choose margarines and spreads that say they are suitable for baking, and avoid 'low fat' types.

Beating butter & sugar

1 Put the sugar and butter in a large mixing bowl. Stir them together with a wooden spoon.

2 Beat quickly with the spoon, until you have a pale, fluffy mixture.

Breaking eggs

Crack the egg sharply on the edge of a bowl. Pull the shell apart, so the white and yolk slide into the bowl. Pick out any bits of shell that fall in.

Beating eggs

Beat the yolk and white with a fork, to mix them together well.

Is it cooked?

At the end of the cooking time, you need to test whether a cake is cooked. Take it out of the oven. Poke the middle of the cake gently with your finger. It should feel firm and springy. If not, bake for 5 minutes more, then test again.

Contains optional nuts

Chocolate peanut brownies

Ingredients:

100g (4oz) salted, roasted peanuts

100g (4oz) plain chocolate

2 large eggs

125g (4½oz) softened butter, margarine or dairy-free spread

275g (10oz) soft light brown sugar

½ teaspoon vanilla essence

50g (2oz) self-raising flour

25g (1oz) plain flour

2 tablespoons cocoa powder

You will also need a 20cm (8in) square cake tin.

Makes 8 to 12

Chocolate and peanuts taste delicious together in these fudgy chocolate brownies. Try them warm with peanut butter sauce and ice cream. For more traditional brownies, use pecans instead of the peanuts, or leave out the nuts altogether.

1 Heat the oven to 180°C, 350°F or gas mark 4. Grease and line the tin (see page 6).

2 Put the peanuts in a sieve and rinse them well under a cold tap, to remove the salt. Then, pat them dry with a clean tea towel.

3 Melt the chocolate, following the instructions on page 36. Wearing oven gloves, take the bowl out of the pan.

4 Break the eggs into a small bowl. Beat them with a fork.

5 Put the butter, margarine or spread, sugar and vanilla in a big bowl. Beat until they are fluffy. Add the beaten eggs a little at a time, beating well each time.

6 Sift both types of flour and the cocoa powder into the bowl. Add the melted chocolate and the peanuts. Mix well.

7 Scrape the mixture into the tin. Smooth the top with the back of a spoon. Bake for 35 minutes, until slightly risen. They will have a crust on top but a soft middle.

8 Leave in the tin for 20 minutes to cool. Then cut into 8-12 pieces.

Peanut butter sauce

Contains nuts

To make a simple peanut butter sauce to eat with your brownies, you will need 150g (5oz) smooth peanut butter. Put it in a small saucepan over a low heat for 5 minutes, stirring every now and then, until the peanut butter becomes soft and runny.

Chocolate orange cookies

Ingredients:

1 orange

75g (3oz) softened butter, margarine or dairy-free spread

75g (3oz) caster sugar

75g (3oz) soft light brown sugar

1 medium egg

1 teaspoon vanilla essence

150g (5oz) plain flour

½ teaspoon baking powder

4 tablespoons cocoa powder

150g (5oz) plain, milk or white chocolate chips

Makes around 24

The recipe for these chocolate cookies is flavoured with orange zest and packed with chocolate chips — or you could use orange sugar-coated chocolate beans.

Only remove the orange layer — the white layer underneath tastes bitter.

1 Heat the oven to 180°C, 350°F or gas mark 4. Grease two baking trays (see page 6). Grate the zest from the outside of the orange, using the small holes of a grater.

2 Put the butter, margarine or spread, both types of sugar and the orange zest in a big bowl. Beat them until the mixture is smooth.

3 Break the egg into a small bowl. Add the vanilla and beat with a fork. Add it to the big bowl a little at a time, beating well each time.

4 Sift the flour, baking powder and cocoa powder into the bowl. Stir the mixture until it is smooth. Add 100g (4oz) of the chocolate chips and stir them in.

5 Take a heaped teaspoon of the mixture and use your hands to roll it into a ball.

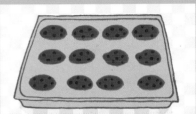

6 Put the ball of dough on the tray and flatten it slightly. Make more cookies with the rest of the mixture. Scatter the rest of the chocolate chips over the cookies and press them on, gently.

7 Bake for 10 minutes. Leave the cookies on the trays for a few minutes, then use a spatula to lift them onto a wire rack to cool.

Other flavours

☆ Replace the chocolate chips with orange chocolate chunks, made by breaking 150g (5oz) orange chocolate into pieces, then cutting them into small chunks with a sharp knife.

☆ For plain choc chip cookies, just leave out the orange zest.

☆ For lemon or lime chocolate cookies, replace the orange zest with the zest of 1 large lemon or 2 limes.

Chocolate cupcakes

Ingredients:

For the cupcakes:

100g (4oz) self-raising flour

40g (1½oz) cocoa powder

1½ teaspoons baking powder

150g (5oz) softened butter, margarine or dairy-free spread

150g (5oz) soft light brown sugar

1 teaspoon vanilla essence

3 tablespoons milk or water

3 large eggs

For the buttercream:

100g (4oz) softened butter, margarine or dairy-free spread

225g (8oz) icing sugar

1 tablespoon milk or water

½ teaspoon vanilla essence

different shades of food dye (optional)

You will also need a 12-hole muffin tray and 12 paper muffin cases.

Makes 12

These chocolate cupcakes are topped with a swirl of buttercream. Decorate them with sugar sprinkles, or look at pages 32, 33 and 37 for more decorating ideas.

1 Heat the oven to 180°C, 350°F or gas mark 4. Put a paper case in each hollow of the tray.

2 Sift the flour, cocoa and baking powder into a big bowl. Put the butter, margarine or spread and sugar in another bowl.

3 Beat the butter, margarine or spread and sugar until they are pale and fluffy. Mix in the vanilla and milk or water.

4 Crack an egg into a cup. Tip it into the butter and sugar mixture. Add 1 tablespoon of the floury mixture. Beat well. Do this with each egg.

5 Add the rest of the floury mixture and stir it in gently, using a big metal spoon.

Move the spoon in the... ...shape of a number 8.

6 Spoon the mixture into the paper cases. Bake for 12-15 minutes, until the cakes are risen and firm. Leave them in the tray for a few minutes. Then, put them on a wire rack to cool.

7 For the buttercream, put the butter, margarine or spread in a bowl. Beat with a wooden spoon until soft. Sift in one third of the icing sugar. Stir it in.

If you're using sugar sprinkles, scatter them on as soon as you've spread on the buttercream.

8 Sift in the rest of the icing sugar. Add the milk or water and vanilla. Beat quickly until the mixture is fluffy. Leave one third of the buttercream, and spoon the rest into two separate bowls.

9 Dye two of the bowls of buttercream, by mixing a couple of drops of food dye into each of them. When the cakes are cool, spread on the buttercream.

Chocolate buttercream

For chocolate buttercream, use just 175g (6oz) icing sugar. At step 8, sift in 40g (1½oz) cocoa powder at the same time as the icing sugar. Leave out the food dye.

13

Chocolate tarts

Ingredients:

For the pastry:

175g (6oz) plain flour

75g (3oz) chilled butter

For the ganache:

200g (7oz) plain chocolate

100ml (3½floz) double cream

You will also need a 12-hole shallow bun tray and a round or wavy cutter around 7cm (2½in) across.

Makes 12

These little pastry tarts are filled with a combination of chocolate and cream, known as ganache. You could use plain, milk or white chocolate ganache (see page 37).

1 Sift the flour into a big bowl. Cut the butter into chunks and stir them into the flour.

2 Pick up some butter and flour in your fingers, and squash and rub them together. Lift the mixture up and let it drop back into the bowl as you rub. Carry on rubbing until the lumps are the size of small breadcrumbs.

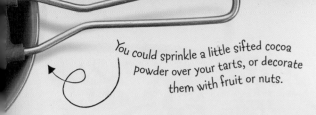

You could sprinkle a little sifted cocoa powder over your tarts, or decorate them with fruit or nuts.

If the mixture feels too dry, add another teaspoon of water.

3 Add 2 tablespoons of cold water to the mixture. Stir it in using a blunt knife, cutting through the mixture, until everything starts to stick together.

4 Pat the pastry into a ball and press gently to flatten it. Cover it with plastic food wrap and put it in the fridge for 20 minutes. This will make it easier to roll out.

5 Heat the oven to 180°C, 350°F or gas mark 4. Make the ganache, following the instructions on page 37. Then, grease the hollows of the bun tray — see page 6.

6 Sprinkle some flour on a clean work surface and a rolling pin. Unwrap the pastry and put it on the floury surface.

7 Roll out the pastry until it is about 30cm (12in) across. Use the cutter to cut out lots of pastry circles.

8 Put one pastry circle over each hollow in the bun tray. Push the circles gently into the hollows.

9 Roll the scraps into a ball. Roll it out again and cut more circles, until you have filled the tray. Use a fork to prick each pastry circle several times.

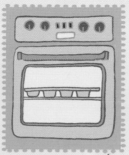

10 Bake for 10-12 minutes until golden brown. Take out of the oven and leave in the tin to cool.

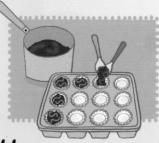

11 Spoon ganache into each pastry case. Put the tarts in the fridge for 30 minutes, to set.

White chocolate cheesecake

Ingredients:

175g (6oz) digestive biscuits
  (gluten-free types are available)

75g (3oz) butter

200g (7oz) white chocolate

400g (14oz) full-fat cream cheese

50g (2oz) caster sugar

2 medium eggs

2 teaspoons vanilla essence

10 strawberries, to decorate

For the raspberry sauce:

150g (5oz) raspberries

50g (2oz) icing sugar

You will also need a 20cm (8in)
round cake tin with a loose base.

This cheesecake is made with white chocolate and decorated with sliced strawberries. There's a recipe for tangy raspberry sauce to pour over it, too.

1 Leave the cream cheese at room temperature for half an hour. Then, heat the oven to 150°C, 300°F or gas mark 2. Grease the tin (see page 6).

2 Put the biscuits in a clean plastic food bag. Seal the end with an elastic band. Roll a rolling pin over it to crush the biscuits into crumbs.

3 Melt the butter in a saucepan over a low heat. Mix in the biscuit crumbs.

4 Spoon the mixture into the tin. Press it down with the back of a spoon. Put the tin in the fridge to chill.

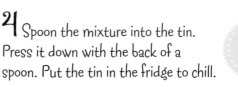

5 Melt the chocolate, following the instructions on page 36.

6 Put the cream cheese and sugar in a big bowl and mix them together. Put the eggs and vanilla in a small bowl. Beat them with a fork.

7 Add the egg mixture to the cheese mixture a little at a time, beating well each time. Then, stir in the melted chocolate.

8 Pour the mixture over the biscuit base. Level the top with the back of a spoon. Bake for 30 minutes. Turn off the oven and leave the cheesecake in for 30 minutes more.

9 Take the cheesecake out of the oven and leave it on a wire rack to cool. Then, put it in the fridge for at least 2 hours.

10 For the raspberry sauce, put the raspberries in a bowl and sift over the icing sugar. Mash everything together with a fork.

11 Take the tin out of the fridge. Put it over a full food can. Press the sides of the tin down around the can. Then, slide the cheesecake off the base of the tin, onto a plate.

You could make lots of white chocolate curls to top your cheesecake — see page 33.

12 Remove the green stalks from the strawberries. Cut the strawberries into thin slices, then press them around the edge of the cheesecake.

Little chocolate puddings

Ingredients:

For the puddings:

75g (3oz) caster sugar

75g (3oz) self-raising flour

1 tablespoon cocoa powder

15g (½oz) butter, margarine or dairy-free spread

4 tablespoons milk

1 teaspoon vanilla essence

For the sauce:

a little soft light brown sugar

a little cocoa powder

a little hot water

You will also need 4 small ovenproof dishes, each with a capacity of around 150ml (¼ pint), and a little icing sugar.

Makes 4

These individual chocolate sponge puddings make their own chocolate sauce as they bake in the oven. You simply sprinkle the sauce ingredients on top before you cook them.

1 Heat the oven to 180°C, 350°F or gas mark 4. Grease the dishes (see page 6). Then, put the dishes on a baking tray.

2 To make the puddings, put the caster sugar in a bowl. Sift in the flour and cocoa powder.

3 Melt the butter, margarine or spread in a small pan over a low heat. Turn off the heat and add the milk and vanilla. Pour the mixture into the bowl.

4 Stir until the mixture is smooth. Then spoon it into the dishes, dividing it equally between them.

5 To make the sauce, sprinkle 2 teaspoons of soft light brown sugar over each dish. Then scatter 1½ teaspoons of cocoa over each dish.

6 Carefully spoon 3 tablespoons of hot water into each dish. Don't worry if the puddings look a little messy.

7 Bake for 15 minutes, until the tops of the puddings are risen and look firm, and all the water has disappeared. Take them out of the oven and leave them to cool for 10 minutes.

8 Sift a little icing sugar over the puddings before you eat them. You will find a pool of chocolate sauce under the sponge in each dish.

Big chocolate pudding

If you prefer, you can make one big chocolate pudding instead of 4 little ones. You will need an ovenproof dish with a capacity of around 600ml (1 pint). At step 4 spoon all the mixture into the dish, then scatter over 3 tablespoons soft light brown sugar, 2 tablespoons cocoa powder and pour on 200ml (7floz) hot water. Bake for 20-25 minutes. Leave to cool for 5 minutes, then sift over a little icing sugar and spoon the pudding into bowls.

Soft-centre cookies

Ingredients:

65g (2½oz) plain chocolate

15g (½oz) butter

1 medium egg

½ teaspoon vanilla essence

40g (1½oz) caster sugar

50g (2oz) self-raising flour

15g (½oz) cocoa powder

50g (2oz) icing sugar

For the filling:

10 squares plain, milk or white chocolate

Makes 10

When you bite into these cookies, you'll discover a surprise chocolate filling. If you eat them when they're still warm, the chocolate filling will be soft and gooey.

1 Fill a pan ¼ full of water and put it over a low heat. When it bubbles, turn off the heat. Put the chocolate in a heatproof bowl. Cut the butter into chunks and add it too.

2 Wearing oven gloves, put the bowl in the pan. Leave for 2 minutes. Stir until the chocolate and butter melt.

3 Break the egg into a small bowl. Add the vanilla and beat them together. Stir into the chocolate mixture.

4 Add the caster sugar and stir for a minute, so the sugar starts to dissolve. Carefully lift the bowl out of the pan and leave the mixture to cool.

5 Sift the flour and cocoa over the mixture. Stir them in. Cover the bowl with plastic food wrap and put it in the fridge for an hour.

6 Heat the oven to 170°C, 325°F or gas mark 3. Line a baking tray with parchment (see page 6). Sift the icing sugar onto a plate.

7 Use a tablespoon to scoop up some mixture. Roll it into a ball with your hands. Make 9 more balls in the same way. Put one on a clean surface and press your thumb into the middle to make a hollow.

8 Press a square of chocolate into the hollow. Use your fingers to pull the dough over the chocolate, to cover it. Shape the cookie into a flattened ball.

As the cookies bake, cracks form on top.

9 Roll the cookie in the icing sugar and put it on the tray. Make the other cookies in the same way.

10 Bake for 10-12 minutes. Leave on the tray for a few minutes, then put them on a wire rack to cool.

Chocolate profiteroles

Ingredients:

For the profiteroles:

50g (2oz) plain flour

15g (½oz) cocoa powder

2 medium eggs

1 teaspoon caster sugar

50g (2oz) butter

For the raspberry cream:

150g (5oz) fresh or frozen
  raspberries

1 teaspoon caster sugar

150ml (¼ pint) double or
  whipping cream

To decorate:

75g (3oz) white chocolate

Makes around 15

Profiteroles are little, crispy pastry puffs. These chocolate puffs are filled with tangy raspberry cream, but you could just use whipped cream if you prefer.

1 Heat the oven to 220°C, 425°F or gas mark 7. Grease two baking trays (see page 6). Hold each tray under the cold tap briefly, then shake off the water.

2 Cut a large rectangle of baking parchment. Fold it in half. Unfold it again. Sift the flour and cocoa onto it. Sprinkle on the sugar. Break the eggs into a small bowl and beat them.

3 Cut the butter into small chunks. Put them in a pan with 150ml (¼ pint) water. Heat gently. As soon as it boils, take it off the heat.

4 Right away, fold up the parchment and tip the flour into the pan. Beat quickly for about a minute, until the mixture begins to form a ball in the middle of the pan.

5 Leave to cool for 5 minutes. Then, add a little egg and stir it in. Add the rest of the egg a little at a time, stirring well each time.

6 Put heaped teaspoons of the mixture onto the baking trays, spacing them well apart.

7 Bake for 10 minutes, then turn down the heat to 190°C, 375°F or gas mark 5. Bake for another 10-12 minutes until they are puffy.

8 Use a spatula to move the puffs onto a wire rack to cool. Then, make a hole in the side of each one with a sharp knife to let out any steam.

9 For the raspberry cream, put the raspberries in a bowl with the sugar and mash them with a fork.

Don't beat too much, or the cream will go hard.

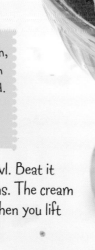

10 Pour the cream into a big bowl. Beat it quickly with a whisk until it thickens. The cream should stand up in a floppy point when you lift the whisk.

11 Add the raspberries. Mix them in very gently with a metal spoon. Melt the white chocolate (see page 36).

12 The puffs should now be cold. Cut a slit in the side of each one. Spoon in some raspberry cream, then drizzle the white chocolate over them.

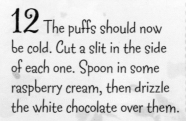

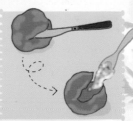

Chocolate macaroons

Ingredients:

100g (4oz) icing sugar

2 medium eggs

1 pinch cream of tartar

25g (1oz) cocoa powder

25g (1oz) caster sugar

75g (3oz) ground almonds

For the ganache:

75g (3oz) plain chocolate

4 tablespoons double cream

Makes around 8 pairs

These chocolate macaroons are crisp, chewy shells, filled with creamy chocolate ganache.

1 Line two large baking trays with baking parchment (see page 6). Sift the icing sugar into a bowl.

You don't need the yolks.

You could use the two egg yolks to replace one egg in the recipes on pages 8, 12, 26, 28 or 30.

2 Break an egg onto a plate. Cover the yolk with an egg cup. Hold the egg cup firmly and tip the plate, so the white slides off into a small bowl. Do the same with the other egg. Put both egg whites in a large, clean bowl.

3 Whisk the egg whites until they become thick and foamy. When you lift up the whisk, the foam should stay in a floppy point.

4 Whisk in the cream of tartar and 2 tablespoons of the icing sugar. Add the rest of the icing sugar, a tablespoon at a time, whisking well each time.

Move the spoon in the...

...shape of a number 8.

Use another spoon to push off each blob.

5 Sift the cocoa over the mixture. Add the caster sugar and ground almonds. Use a metal spoon to fold everything together very gently.

6 Scoop up a teaspoon of the mixture and put it on a tray. Put more blobs on the trays, spacing them out well.

7 Tap each tray sharply on the work surface, twice. Leave for 30 minutes. Make the ganache, following the instructions on page 37.

8 Heat the oven to 110°C, 225°F or gas mark ¼. Bake for 30 minutes. Turn off the oven and leave them in for 15 minutes. Then leave them on the trays to cool.

9 Spread some ganache onto the flat side of a macaroon. Press on another macaroon. Fill all the macaroons the same way.

This macaroon was decorated using a stencil and coloured icing sugar (see page 32).

White chocolate gateau

Ingredients:

For the cake:

100g (4oz) self-raising flour

40g (1½oz) cocoa powder

1½ teaspoons baking powder

150g (5oz) softened butter or margarine

150g (5oz) soft light brown sugar

1 teaspoon vanilla essence

3 tablespoons milk or water

3 large eggs

For the white chocolate mousse:

200g (7oz) white chocolate

300ml (½ pint) whipping cream

You will also need lots of white chocolate-covered finger biscuits for decorating, and a round cake tin, preferably 18cm (7in) across, but a 20cm (8in) one will do.

This impressive gateau is perfect for celebrations. It is made with chocolate cake and decorated with white chocolate mousse and white chocolate finger biscuits.

1 Heat the oven to 180°C, 350°F or gas mark 4. Grease and line the tin (see page 6).

Peel off the parchment when the cake is cool.

2 To make the cake, follow steps 2-5 on page 12. Scrape the mix into the tin. Level the top with the back of a spoon. Bake for 30-35 minutes until risen and springy. Leave in the tin for a few minutes.

3 Hold the tin upside down over a wire rack. Shake the tin, so the cake pops out. Leave it to cool.

4 To make the white chocolate mousse, follow steps 1 and 3-6 on pages 44-45.

5 Use a knife to spread some white chocolate mousse onto the sides of cake.

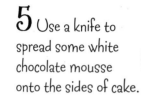

6 Press the white chocolate fingers around the sides of the cake. Spoon the rest of the mousse on top of the cake. Put in the fridge for at least 1 hour.

You could decorate your gateau with fresh berries and chocolate curls – see page 33.

Other toppings

Sliced peaches or apricots make a good topping for your gateau, too. Or, instead of fruit, pile on some home-made truffles (page 48) or chocolate paste shapes (page 33).

Milk or plain chocolate

Instead of using white chocolate to make the mousse, you could replace it with milk or plain chocolate. Decorate the sides of the gateau with milk or plain chocolate finger biscuits.

Chocolate lime surprise cake

Ingredients:

For the cake:

2 limes

175g (6oz) softened butter or margarine

175g (6oz) caster sugar

3 medium eggs

2 tablespoons cocoa powder

1 teaspoon baking powder

200g (7oz) self-raising flour

5 tablespoons plain yogurt

1 pinch chilli flakes (optional)

For the ganache topping:

100g (4oz) plain chocolate

100g (4oz) milk chocolate

150ml (¼ pint) sour cream

You will also need a 20cm (8in) round cake tin, at least 7cm (3in) deep.

The surprise ingredient in this moist chocolate and lime cake is a pinch of chilli. It adds just a subtle hint of heat, but you can leave it out if you prefer.

1 Heat the oven to 170°C, 325°F or gas mark 3. Grease and line the tin (see page 6).

Only remove the green layer – the white layer underneath tastes bitter.

2 Grate the zest from the outside of the limes, using the small holes of the grater. Cut the limes in half and squeeze out the juice.

3 Put the butter or margarine, sugar and zest in a big bowl. Beat until the mixture is light and fluffy.

4 Break the eggs into a small bowl. Mix with a fork. Put a spoonful in the big bowl. Beat it in well. Add the rest of the egg, a spoonful at a time, beating well each time.

5 Put the cocoa powder in a cup. Stir in 2 tablespoons of warm water to make a smooth paste. Put it in the big bowl and stir it in.

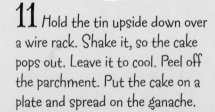

You could decorate your cake with lime zest.

6 Sift in the baking powder and about half the flour. Gently fold the ingredients together with a metal spoon. Then add the yogurt and fold it in.

Move the spoon in the...

...shape of a number 8.

7 Sift in the remaining flour. Add the lime juice and chilli flakes. Stir the ingredients together very gently.

These little curls of zest were made by scraping a tool called a zester across the surface of a lime.

8 Spoon the mixture into the tin. Smooth the top with the back of a spoon. Bake for 1 hour, until the cake is firm and springy.

9 Make the ganache following the instructions on page 37.

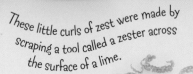

10 When the cake is cooked, leave it in the tin for a few minutes. Run a knife around the edge of the tin.

11 Hold the tin upside down over a wire rack. Shake it, so the cake pops out. Leave it to cool. Peel off the parchment. Put the cake on a plate and spread on the ganache.

Chocolate traybake

Ingredients:

For the cake:

225g (8oz) softened butter, margarine or dairy-free spread

225g (8oz) caster sugar

4 medium eggs

50g (2oz) cocoa powder

2 teaspoons gluten-free baking powder

165g (5½oz) fine cornmeal (polenta)

1 teaspoon vanilla essence

For decorating:

100g (4oz) allergy-free white chocolate chips, or allergy-free white chocolate chopped into tiny chunks

50g (2oz) allergy-free plain chocolate chips, or allergy-free plain chocolate chopped into tiny chunks

You will also need a 27 x 18cm (11 x 7in) rectangular cake tin.

Makes around 12 squares

This simple chocolate cake doesn't contain any wheat, gluten or nuts, and you can make it dairy-free too, so as well as being delicious, it's a good choice if you're cooking for someone who can't eat those foods.

1 Heat the oven to 190°C, 375°F or gas mark 5. Grease and line the tin (see page 6).

2 Beat the butter, margarine or dairy-free spread and sugar together in a large bowl, until they are pale and fluffy.

3 Break the eggs into a small bowl and beat them with a fork. Add them to the beaten mixture a little at a time, beating it again after each addition.

You could decorate your finished traybake with chocolate paste shapes – see page 33.

Peel off the parchment.

4 Sift the cocoa and baking powder into the bowl. Add the cornmeal, vanilla and a tablespoon of water. Mix well.

5 Spoon the mixture into the tin, pushing it into the corners with the back of a spoon. Bake for 25-30 minutes until the cake is firm and springy. Leave for 5 minutes, to cool.

6 Shake the tin upside down over a wire rack. The cake should pop out. While it is still hot, make the marbled chocolate topping (see page 37).

7 When the topping has set, put the cake on a board, then cut it into around 12 squares.

Tips for decorating

Here you'll find instructions for making decorations, including home-made chocolate buttons, to adorn your chocolate confections.

Coloured icing sugar

You will need some icing sugar and a little food dye.

1 Put 1 tablespoon of the sugar on a plate. Mix in a few drops of food dye. Scrape the mixture into a sieve. Use a spoon to press it through the sieve into a small bowl. Tip the mixture back into the sieve and press it through again, and then a third time.

2 Spread out the sugar and leave it to dry for around 2 hours. When the sugar is dry, press it through a clean sieve one last time. Then, it is ready to use.

Stencilled cake decorations

You will need some icing sugar or cocoa powder and a piece of paper bigger than the cakes or tarts you want to decorate.

1 Fold the paper in half. Draw half a heart (or other shape) against the fold. Cut along the line, then unfold the paper.

2 Attach a loop of sticky tape to the heart or other shape. Put the shape on a cake or tart. Put the paper with the hole in it on another.

3 Sift a little icing sugar or cocoa over the cakes or tarts. Carefully remove the stencils.

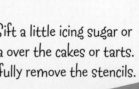

Coloured icing sugar

Chocolate paste

You will need 75g (3oz) plain, milk or white chocolate and 1½ tablespoons golden syrup.

1 Melt the chocolate (see page 36). Wearing oven gloves, take the bowl out of the pan. Leave for 2 minutes to cool.

2 Add the golden syrup. Stir until the mixture forms a thick paste that doesn't stick to the sides of the bowl. Pat it into a flattened ball.

3 Wrap it in plastic food wrap and put it in the fridge for 1 hour. Take it out of the fridge and leave it to soften for 10 minutes.

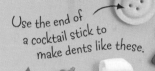

Use the end of a cocktail stick to make dents like these.

Chocolate paste decorations

To make balls, roll a piece of chocolate paste between the palms of your hands, like this. To make a circle, squash the ball with your thumb or finger.

To make a chocolate paste button, first make a circle of paste. Press a clean button onto the circle. Then, carefully take off the button.

To cut shapes from chocolate paste, dust a surface and rolling pin with a little cocoa powder or icing sugar. Roll out the paste until it's half as thin as your little finger.

Cut out shapes using small cookie cutters. Squeeze the scraps together, roll them out and cut out more shapes.

Chocolate curls

You will need a bar of chocolate that's at room temperature.

Scrape strips from the side of the bar using a vegetable peeler.

For wider curls, break the bar into strips. Scrape the peeler along the back of the strips.

You'll find a recipe for chocolate fondue on pages 46-47.

Melting chocolate

Tips for melting chocolate

Here you'll find some tips to help you when you're melting chocolate, and recipes for toppings and fillings for cakes and other things.

About melting chocolate

When you melt chocolate and then let it set again, it becomes softer and less glossy. To stop this from happening, professional chocolatiers 'temper' chocolate – they heat and cool it very precisely.

You don't need to temper chocolate for any of the recipes in this book, but it's best to use the method for melting shown here. You can melt chocolate in a microwave, but this heats it too fiercely for the recipes in this book.

Melting chocolate

1 For best results, find a heatproof bowl that fits snugly in a saucepan, so that the bottom of the bowl doesn't touch the bottom of the pan, and there's a gap of around 5cm (2in) between them.

2 Fill the pan with water to a depth of around 4cm (1½in). Put it over a medium heat. When the water bubbles, take it off the heat.

3 Break up the chocolate. Put it in the bowl. Wearing oven gloves, lower the bowl into the pan. Leave for 5 minutes. Stir until the chocolate melts.

For cooking, you can use chocolate chips or chocolate from a bar. If you buy chocolate in bars you have more choice of different types of chocolate.

Drizzling melted chocolate

1 Melt 75g (3oz) plain, milk or white chocolate following the instructions on the opposite page.

2 Scoop up some melted chocolate. Hold the spoon over a lollipop or cake. Tip the spoon, then move it over the lollipop or cake, leaving a trail of chocolate.

Marbled chocolate topping

To make a marbled topping on a cake, you will need 100g (4oz) white chocolate chips and 50g (2oz) plain chocolate chips.

1 While the cake is still hot, sprinkle the white and plain chocolate chips over the cake. Leave them for 5 minutes to melt.

2 Use the back of a teaspoon to swirl the chocolate gently into a marbled pattern. Put the cake in the fridge until the topping has set.

Ganache

Ganache is a creamy, chocolatey filling or topping. You will need 200g (7oz) plain or milk chocolate and 100ml (3½floz) double cream.

1 Melt the chocolate (see opposite). Stir in the cream. Wearing oven gloves, take the bowl out of the pan.

2 Let it cool for 10 minutes, then put it in the fridge for 1 hour. Stir every now and then.

To make white chocolate ganache, replace the plain or milk chocolate with 300g (11oz) white chocolate.

You can make ganache with sour cream instead of double cream, for a slightly sharper flavour.

Chocolate lollipops

Ingredients:

100g (4oz) unsalted nuts, such as pecans, walnuts, pistachios or chopped nuts (optional)

75g (3oz) plain chocolate

75g (3oz) white chocolate

You will also need 2 baking trays and around 18-20 cocktail sticks, wooden skewers, or other lollipop sticks.

Makes around 18-20

Chocolate lollipops are very easy to make. You can decorate them with nuts or other toppings such as drizzled chocolate or sugar sprinkles.

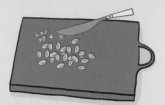

1 Line the trays with baking parchment (see page 6). If you are using whole nuts, put them on a chopping board and carefully cut each one into small pieces using a sharp knife.

2 Melt the plain chocolate following the instructions on page 36. Wearing oven gloves, take the bowl out of the pan. Spoon a teaspoon of chocolate onto a tray. Use the spoon to smooth it into a circle.

3 Press a lollipop stick into the chocolate. Use the back of the spoon to smooth the chocolate over the stick.

4 Make more lollipops. Sprinkle half the nuts over them. Then, melt the white chocolate and make more lollipops in the same way.

5 Put the trays in the fridge for half an hour to set. Then, carefully peel the lollipops off the parchment.

Other toppings

☆ For fruity lollipops, replace the nuts with 50g (2oz) dried fruit such as apricots, mango, papaya, cranberries or cherries.

☆ Melt 40g (1½oz) chocolate and drizzle it over your finished lollipops. See page 37 for instructions. Contrasting colours of chocolate look best.

☆ Sprinkle 2 tablespoons of sugar sprinkles over the lollipops at step 4, instead of the nuts.

This lollipop was only drizzled with white chocolate.

Mint hot chocolate

This recipe is for a luxurious hot chocolate drink made with melted chocolate, whipped cream and a refreshing taste of mint. The opposite page also shows you how to make plain hot chocolate, or add different flavours.

Ingredients:

75ml (3floz) whipping cream (optional)

100g (4oz) plain chocolate

450ml (¾ pint) milk

4 drops peppermint essence

1 teaspoon caster sugar

Makes 4 cups

Don't beat too much, or the cream will go hard.

1 Pour the cream into a large bowl. Whisk the cream quickly until it thickens. The cream should stay in a floppy point when you lift the whisk.

2 Break the chocolate into a saucepan. Add the milk, peppermint essence and sugar. Then, heat it gently, stirring all the time.

3 When the chocolate has melted, beat the mixture with a whisk until it just starts to boil and is creamy and frothy.

4 Take the pan off the heat. Pour the hot chocolate into 4 cups and spoon on the cream.

Decorate your mint hot chocolate with fresh mint leaves.

Other flavours

☆ To make plain hot chocolate or other flavours of hot chocolate, leave out the peppermint essence in step 1.

☆ For cinnamon hot chocolate, add a pinch of ground cinnamon in step 1. You could sprinkle another pinch of ground cinnamon over the finished hot chocolate.

☆ Mocha is a name for combined coffee and chocolate flavours. For hot mocha, add a teaspoon of instant coffee in step 1.

☆ You could use milk or white chocolate instead of plain chocolate, but leave out the sugar, as they are sweet enough.

☆ For chilli hot chocolate, add a pinch of chilli flakes in step 1. When you pour the hot chocolate into the cups at step 3, pour it through a strainer.

☆ For orange hot chocolate, use a vegetable peeler to peel three strips of zest from an orange. Add them to the pan in step 1. When you pour the hot chocolate into the cups, pour it through a strainer.

You could finish your cinnamon hot chocolate with a cinnamon stick, for stirring.

See page 33 to find out how to make white chocolate curls to decorate a cup of white hot chocolate.

41

Choc-mallow ice cream

Ingredients:

300ml (½ pint) milk

175g (6oz) marshmallows

200g (7oz) plain chocolate

300ml (½ pint) double cream

You will also need 2 freezer-proof containers with tightly-fitting lids.

Serves 8

This chocolate ice cream is made with melted chocolate and marshmallows. The finished ice cream tastes even more delicious with chocolate sauce made using the recipe on the opposite page.

1 Pour the milk into a saucepan. Add the marshmallows. Put the pan over a medium heat.

Don't let the mixture boil.

2 Stir every now and then, until the marshmallows have nearly melted. Turn off the heat, but leave the pan where it is.

3 Break up the chocolate. Put it in the pan. Leave for 2-3 minutes. Stir until the chocolate and marshmallows have melted. Leave the mixture to cool.

Don't beat too much, or the cream will go hard.

4 Pour the cream into a bowl. Whisk the cream quickly until it thickens. The cream should stand up in a floppy point when you lift the whisk.

5 Pour the chocolate mixture into the cream. Mix everything together gently, moving the spoon in the shape of a number 8.

6 Pour the mixture into the containers and put on the lids. Put them in the freezer for 4-5 hours until the ice cream is firm.

It's fine to freeze your ice cream for longer, but it will become rather hard to scoop. You can soften it a little by putting it in the fridge 15 minutes before you want to scoop it.

Chocolate sauce

To make chocolate sauce for the ice cream, put 2 tablespoons
of cream cheese or mascarpone cheese into a small pan. Heat it
gently for 5 minutes, until it melts. Take the pan off the heat and
add 2 squares of chocolate. Mix until the chocolate melts.

You could sprinkle extra mini marshmallows
over your finished ice cream, if you like.

It's not a good idea to
re-freeze ice cream when it's
been out of the freezer for a
while. This ice cream is frozen
in 2 separate portions, so you
can eat one and leave the
second one in the freezer for
another day, if you like.

Chocolate berry mousse

Ingredients:

100g (4oz) white chocolate

150g (5oz) fresh or frozen raspberries

150ml (¼ pint) whipping cream

You will also need 4-6 small glasses, dishes or teacups.

Makes 4-6 pots

This recipe is for a creamy white chocolate mousse, swirled with crushed raspberries. There are also other flavour combinations you could try – you'll find some ideas on the page opposite.

1 Melt the chocolate, following the instructions on page 36. Take the bowl out of the pan, wearing oven gloves.

Don't beat too much, or the cream will go hard.

2 Put the raspberries in a bowl and mash them with a fork until some of them are squashed and juicy.

3 Pour the cream into a large bowl. Beat it very quickly with a whisk.

4 Carry on beating until the cream stands up in a floppy point when you lift up the whisk, like this.

Don't worry if it looks a bit lumpy at this stage.

5 Add a large spoonful of the cream to the melted chocolate. Stir it in gently with a metal spoon, moving it in the shape of a number 8.

6 Add the rest of the whipped cream. Stir gently with the metal spoon again, until it is all mixed in.

7 Add the raspberries. Move the metal spoon through the mixture, so they start to mix in. Stop when the mixture is swirled with pink.

8 Spoon the mousse into the glasses or dishes. Put them in the fridge for at least 1 hour.

Other flavours

For milk or plain chocolate mousse, simply replace the white chocolate with milk or plain. You could also replace the raspberries with other berries such as blueberries, ripe strawberries, or cherries with the stones removed.

Contains optional nuts

Chocolate fondue

Ingredients:

Around 450g (1lb) fresh fruit for dipping, such as berries, grapes, apples or bananas

a little lemon juice

around 50g (2oz) chopped nuts, desiccated coconut or sugar sprinkles

200g (7oz) plain chocolate

150ml (¼ pint) double cream

½ teaspoon ground cinnamon (optional)

Serves 4-8

A little ground cinnamon gives this chocolate fondue a hint of spice, but for a plainer chocolate fondue you could just leave it out.

1 First, prepare the fruit. Cut apples into quarters, remove the cores, then cut the apple into bite-sized pieces. Peel bananas and cut them into bite-sized pieces.

2 Put the apple or banana pieces in a bowl. Add half a teaspoon of lemon juice per apple or banana and mix to coat the fruit in the juice. This will stop it from going brown.

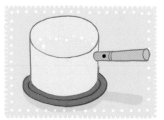

3 Cut up other large fruits into bite-sized pieces. For small fruits such as grapes or berries, remove any stalks. Arrange the fruit in a bowl. Put the nuts, coconut or sprinkles on a plate.

4 Break the chocolate into small chunks. Put the cream and cinnamon in a saucepan.

5 Put the pan over a medium heat. Leave it until the cream steams and small bubbles form around the edge. Take the pan off the heat.

6 Stir in the chocolate until it melts and you have a smooth mixture. Then, pour it into a bowl.

7 Spear a piece of fruit on a fork or skewer and dip it into the fondue. Then, dip the chocolatey fruit into the nuts, coconut or sprinkles, if you like.

Other flavours

You could replace the plain chocolate with milk chocolate. Or, replace the ground cinnamon with a pinch of chilli flakes for a slightly spicy fondue.

Other things to dip

☆ Instead of or as well as fruit, you could dip mini breadsticks, marshmallows, or cubes of bread or plain cake into your chocolate fondue.

☆ You could also dip dried fruit, such as dried apple, mango, dates, apricots or figs.

You could dip other types of fresh fruit, such as the fresh figs used here.

Contains optional nuts

Chocolate truffles

These simple truffles are made from ganache. You can make them with plain, milk or white chocolate and add different flavours and coatings.

Ingredients:

200g (7oz) plain, milk or white chocolate

5 tablespoons double cream

½ teaspoon vanilla essence

You will also need one or more coatings such as sugar strands, desiccated coconut, cocoa, finely chopped nuts or icing sugar.

Makes around 12

1 Make the ganache following step 1 on page 37. Add the vanilla. Let the mixture cool for 10 minutes, then put it in the fridge for 1 hour. Stir every now and then.

4 Put the truffles on a plate. Make more truffles with the rest of the mixture. Put them in the fridge until you are ready to eat them.

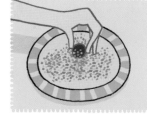

2 Spread each different type of coating onto a plate.

3 Use a teaspoon to scoop up some of the chocolate mixture. Use your hands to roll it quickly into a ball. Then roll the ball in one of the coatings.

Other flavours

To make other flavours of truffles, leave out the vanilla and instead add one of the following in step 1:

☆ 2 drops peppermint essence
☆ a handful chopped dried fruits, such as apricots
☆ ½ teaspoon ground cinnamon
☆ the grated zest of a lime or of half an orange or lemon

With some coatings, the truffle shows through.

Each of these truffles was rolled in a different coating.

Coloured icing sugar (see page 32)

Chocolate strands

Pink sugar crystals

Cocoa powder

Sugar sprinkles

Chopped nuts

Desiccated coconut

This truffle was dipped in milk chocolate and then drizzled with white chocolate.

Chocolate-coated truffles

1 Make the truffles following steps 1 and 3, but don't roll them in a coating. Put them in the fridge, then melt 200g (7oz) chocolate following the steps on page 36.

2 Take the truffles out of the fridge. Push a fork into a truffle and dip it in the melted chocolate. Use a teaspoon to spoon chocolate all over the truffle.

3 Use the spoon to push the truffle gently off the fork and onto the plate. Coat all the truffles in the same way, then put them in the fridge until the chocolate has set.

Rocky road

Rocky road is made from marshmallows mixed with nuts or biscuits and melted chocolate. It sets in the fridge and is sliced into crunchy squares.

Ingredients:

200g (7oz) plain chocolate

85g (3½oz) butter, margarine or dairy-free spread

1 tablespoon golden syrup

85g (3½oz) digestive biscuits (gluten-free types are available) or 200g (7oz) blanched hazelnuts

125g (4½oz) marshmallows, preferably mini ones

You will also need a cake tin or plastic box around 18cm (7in) wide, and some kitchen foil or plastic food wrap.

Makes 12-16 squares

1 Line the tin or box with the foil or wrap, so the bottom and the sides are covered.

2 Break the chocolate into pieces and cut up the butter, margarine or spread into small chunks. Put them in a heatproof bowl with the golden syrup.

3 Fill a pan ¼ full with water. Put it over a gentle heat. When it bubbles, turn off the heat. Wearing oven gloves, put the bowl into the pan. Leave for 2 minutes.

4 After 2 minutes, stir until the chocolate and butter melt. Lift the bowl out of the pan, wearing oven gloves. If you're using biscuits, crumble them into small pieces.

5 Put the biscuits or nuts in the bowl. If you're using mini marshmallows, add them too. If you're using big marshmallows, cut each one into 4 pieces before you add them.

6 Mix well. Spoon the mixture into the box. Use the spoon to push it into the corners. Put it in the fridge for at least 2 hours to chill.

7 Put an upside-down plate over the box. Tip the plate and box over together. Take off the box — you may need to pull on the foil or food wrap.

Rocky road gets its name because the rough, chocolatey top looks a little like a bumpy road strewn with rocks.

This rocky road was made using multicoloured mini marshmallows.

8 Peel off all the foil or wrap. Then, turn the rocky road the right way up again and cut it into lots of little squares.

Other flavours

If you're making your rocky road with soft margarine or dairy-free spread, it won't set really hard, so eat it straight from the fridge.

You can use this recipe to make chocolate cornflake crunch instead of rocky road. Replace the marshmallows and nuts with 100g (4oz) cornflakes. Follow steps 6-8 to make cornflake crunch squares, or spoon the mixture into 12 paper cake cases after step 5.

Chocolate chilli

Ingredients:

1 onion

1 red pepper

450g (1lb) lean braising beef

2 tablespoons olive oil

1 clove of garlic

3 large pinches chilli flakes

1 teaspoon paprika

½ teaspoon dried oregano

½ teaspoon ground cinnamon

1 beef stock cube

a 400g (14oz) can chopped tomatoes

3 tablespoons tomato purée

a 400g (14oz) can red kidney beans

2 teaspoons cocoa powder or 4 squares plain chocolate

Serves 4

You can even use chocolate in some savoury recipes. This beef chilli contains a little chocolate or cocoa powder – it gives it a richer texture and flavour.

1 Cut the ends off the onion and peel it. Cut it in half, cut the halves into slices and the slices into small pieces.

2 Cut the top off the pepper and throw it away. Cut the pepper in half. Pull out the seeds and white parts and throw them away. Cut the pepper into bite-sized pieces.

3 Using a sharp knife, carefully cut the beef into small pieces, about 1½cm (⅝in) across. Cut off any white fat and throw it away.

Stir often as the ingredients cook.

4 Put the oil in a large pan over a high heat. Add the beef and cook for 5 minutes until it is brown all over. Add the onion and pepper. Turn the heat to medium and cook for 5 minutes more.

5 Crush the garlic into the pan. Add the chilli flakes, paprika, oregano and cinnamon. Cook for 1 minute, stirring.

6 Put the stock cube in a heatproof jug. Pour in 300ml (½ pint) of boiling water and stir until the cube dissolves. Pour the stock into the pan. Add the tomatoes and tomato purée.

7 Heat until the mixture boils. Then turn down the heat so it just bubbles. Put a lid on the pan, leaving a small gap. Cook for 40 minutes.

8 Rinse the kidney beans in a sieve under a cold tap. Shake off the excess water. Put the beans in the pan. Stir in the cocoa powder or chocolate. Cook without a lid for 15 minutes.

Eat your chilli with tortilla chips. You could add some sour cream, chopped coriander and a lime wedge to squeeze over it.

Minced beef

Instead of using chunks of beef, you could use 450g (1lb) lean minced beef. Brown it in the pan at step 4, as normal. In step 7, cook the chilli for just 30 minutes.

About chocolate

What is chocolate?

Chocolate is made from the pods of the cacao tree, which grows in hot, rainy areas of the world.

From bean to bar

Inside cacao pods are beans. These are ground to produce a dark brown, bitter paste known as cocoa mass.

To make chocolate, cocoa mass is sweetened with sugar. For some types of chocolate, other ingredients such as milk are added, too. The cocoa mass in solid chocolate is known as cocoa solids.

The pods of the cacao tree grow out of the trunk and branches.

This is unsweetened chocolate, made from cocoa mass with nothing added. It tastes very strong and bitter.

Cacao beans

Cocoa butter

Cocoa powder

Some cocoa mass isn't made into chocolate. Instead, it is processed further, to separate it into dry cocoa powder and fatty cocoa butter.

Cocoa powder has an intense chocolatey taste, but like cocoa mass, it is very bitter. It is used in drinks and cooking. Sugar is usually added, to sweeten it.

Cocoa butter doesn't have a strong taste, but it has a very smooth texture. It is mixed with sugar and other things to make white chocolate, and added to other types of chocolate to make them smoother. The higher the percentage of cocoa butter, the more easily the chocolate melts.

Milk chocolate is great for recipes such as truffles and lollipops.

Plain chocolate has a rich flavour, making it ideal for baking.

Plain chocolate

Plain chocolate, also called bittersweet, Continental or dark chocolate, contains at least 45% cocoa solids, with added sugar, vanilla, and sometimes a little milk or cocoa butter. The higher the percentage of cocoa solids, the stronger the flavour.

Milk chocolate

Milk chocolate contains at least 25% cocoa solids, combined with sugar, vanilla, a higher proportion of milk products (such as cream and milk) and cocoa butter. This gives it a creamier texture and a distinctive, chocolatey flavour that is not as strong as plain chocolate.

White chocolate

White chocolate doesn't contain any cocoa solids, so it isn't really chocolate at all. It is made of at least 20% cocoa butter, as well as milk, sugar and vanilla. It tastes of vanilla, not chocolate, and is very sweet and creamy.

Scientists believe that a small amount of very dark chocolate (containing high cocoa solids) may actually be good for you. They have found that the natural chemicals in cocoa solids may be good for your heart, help you to stay alert and happy, and boost your memory.

How chocolate is made

Turning the bitter beans of the cacao tree into a delicious bar of chocolate is a long process, with many different stages.

Cacao pods contain pulp and beans.

1 Pickers cut the pods from cacao trees using long-handled knives. The pods are split open and the beans and pulp are scooped out.

2 Workers tip the beans and pulp into a heap. When the pulp comes into contact with the air, it starts to heat up and rot, or ferment. The beans change from beige to a rich shade of brown and develop a chocolatey flavour.

The beans and pulp are left for around a week.

The beans are dried on bamboo mats.

3 The beans are spread out and left to dry in the sun, or under hot-air pipes. After a few days, they're ready to be shipped to a chocolate factory.

The beans roast in here.

4 At a chocolate factory, the beans are cleaned and sorted according to their quality, then roasted in huge ovens to bring out an even more chocolatey taste and smell.

5 Next the beans go into a winnowing machine which removes the shells and leaves broken pieces of cacao bean, called nibs. These are ground into a thick paste known as cocoa mass.

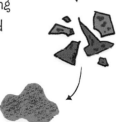

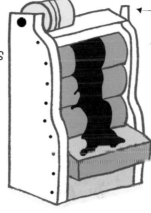

6 Sugar, vanilla and other ingredients are added to the cocoa mass. The mixture is pumped through heavy rollers that grind it into a smooth paste.

7 Next, the paste goes through a machine known as a conching machine. This swirls and mixes the paste until it becomes really thick and velvety.

8 Finally, the chocolate is tempered, by heating and stirring it, to make it smooth and glossy. Then it's squirted into moulds to form bars or other shapes.

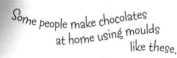

Some people make chocolates at home using moulds like these.

The history of chocolate

No one really knows how chocolate was discovered, but people have been enjoying it for thousands of years.

Mexican discovery

Honey

Historians think the Olmec people, who lived in Mexico 3,000 years ago, first realized that bitter cacao beans could be made into a cold drink. The Maya people, who lived 2,500 years ago, liked to drink cacao hot, mixed with herbs, spices, chilli and sometimes honey. They poured the drink back and forth between a cup and a pot to make it foamy.

Chilli

Vanilla

Allspice

Chilli powder

The scientific name for the cacao tree is *Theobroma cacao*. *Theobroma* means 'food of the gods' in ancient Greek.

Sweet chocolate

In the mid 1500s, the Spanish took control of Mexico. They also governed many Caribbean islands, where they grew sugar. They combined the cacao and sugar, and took the new sweetened recipe back to Spain. The drink eventually reached other European countries and people started to grow cacao trees in the Caribbean, Asia and Central and South America.

Spanish nuns in 16th century Mexico created a savoury chocolate sauce called *mole* (pronounced mo-lay). Served with meat, it is the Mexican national dish.

Hot chocolate

Hot chocolate was an expensive luxury and was fashionable among European royalty. In England and the Netherlands, shopkeepers started to sell the new drink to the public, but still only the wealthy could afford it.

Mass production

By the 1700s, inventors found that new mechanical mills could grind huge amounts of cacao and mass-produce chocolate cheaply and quickly.

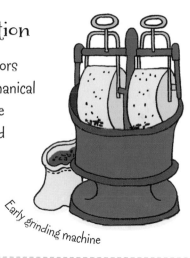

Early grinding machine

Milk chocolate was invented in 1875.

Chocolate bars have been around since 1847.

☆ In the early 1800s, a Dutch scientist, named Conrad van Houten, worked out how to make cocoa powder less bitter.

☆ In 1847, an English chocolate-maker, Joseph Fry, found out how to make a chocolate paste that could be shaped and hardened into a chocolate bar.

☆ In 1875, Swiss food manufacturers Daniel Peter and Henri Nestlé added condensed milk to solid chocolate, inventing milk chocolate.

☆ In 1879, Swiss chocolate-maker Rodolphe Lindt invented a machine to mix chocolate to a very smooth consistency.

The future of chocolate

Food technicians are working all the time to develop new forms of chocolate, including elastic chocolate that can be bent into any shape. Who knows what amazing chocolate creations people will come up with in the future?

Chocolate-makers around the world have come up with thousands of different shapes, sizes and flavours of chocolates.

Index

Allergy advice

Many of the recipes in this book already have clearly-marked optional ingredients, such as nuts, which you can leave out if you're cooking for someone who's allergic to them. There are also suggestions in the ingredients lists for allergy-free ingredients you can substitute, for example using dairy-free spread instead of butter. The list below will tell you about any ingredients that can't be substituted, but might be a problem for those who can't eat wheat, gluten, dairy, egg or nuts.

If you're cooking for someone with food allergies, you should use allergy-free chocolate, which is free from wheat, gluten, egg, nuts and, sometimes, dairy. You should also check any packaged ingredients, such as vanilla, stock cubes, cocoa powder or sugar sprinkles, to make sure they don't contain anything unsuitable.

Chocolate peanut brownies
Contain wheat, gluten, egg and optional nuts. The optional peanut butter sauce contains nuts.

Chocolate orange cookies
Contain wheat, gluten and egg.

Chocolate cupcakes
Contain wheat, gluten and egg.

Chocolate tarts
Contain wheat, gluten and dairy.

White chocolate cheesecake
Contains dairy and eggs.

Little chocolate puddings
Contain wheat, gluten and dairy.

Soft-centre cookies
Contain wheat, gluten, dairy and egg.

Chocolate profiteroles
Contain wheat, gluten, dairy and egg.

Chocolate macaroons
Contain nuts and egg.
The ganache filling contains dairy.

White chocolate gateau
Contains wheat, gluten, dairy and egg.

Chocolate lime surprise cake
Contains wheat, gluten, dairy and egg.

Chocolate traybake
Contains egg.

Chocolate lollipops
Contain optional nuts.

Mint hot chocolate
Contains dairy.

Choc-mallow ice cream
Contains dairy.

Chocolate berry mousse
Contains dairy.

Chocolate fondue
Contains dairy.

Chocolate truffles
Contain dairy and optional nuts.

Rocky road
Contains optional nuts.

Chocolate chilli
Contains no wheat, gluten, egg, nuts or dairy.

Art Director: Mary Cartwright
Digital imaging by Nick Wakeford   Food preparation by Dagmar Vesely